Chapter 1

A fly went flying.

He was looking
for something to eat –

something tasty,

something slimy.

A boy went walking.

He was looking for something to catch – something clever, something for

The Amazing Pet Show.

They met.

The boy caught the fly
in a jar.
"A pet!" he said.

The fly was angry.
He wanted to be free.
He stomped his foot
and said – BUZZ!

The boy was surprised.
He said, "You know my
name! You are the cleverest
pet in the world!"

Chapter 2

Buzz took the fly home.

"This is my pet," Buzz said
to Mum and Dad.

"He is clever. He can say my name. Listen!"

Buzz opened the jar.
The fly flew out.

"Flies can't be pets!" said Dad.
"They are pests!"
He got the fly swatter.
The fly cried —

BUZZ!

And Buzz came to the rescue.
"You are right," said Dad.
"This fly _is_ clever!"

"He needs a name," said Mum.
Buzz thought for a minute.
"Fly Guy," said Buzz.
And Fly Guy said — BUZZ!

It was time for lunch.
Buzz gave Fly Guy
something to eat.

Fly Guy was happy.

Chapter 3

Buzz took Fly Guy to
The Amazing Pet Show.

The judges laughed. "Flies can't be pets," they said. "Flies are pests!"

Buzz was sad.
He opened the jar.
"Shoo, Fly Guy," he said.
"Flies can't be pets."

But Fly Guy liked Buzz.
He had an idea.
He did some fancy flying.

The judges were amazed.
"The fly can do tricks," they said.
"But flies can't be pets."

Then Fly Guy said —

The judges were more amazed. "The fly knows the boy's name," they said. "But flies can't be pets."

Fly Guy flew high, high, high into the sky!

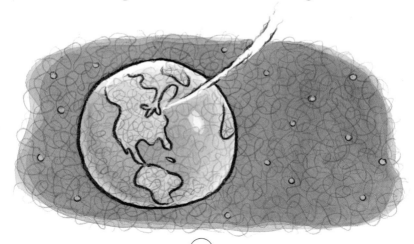

Then he dived down, down, down into the jar.

"The fly knows his jar!" the judges said. "This fly <u>is</u> a pet!" They let Fly Guy be in the show.

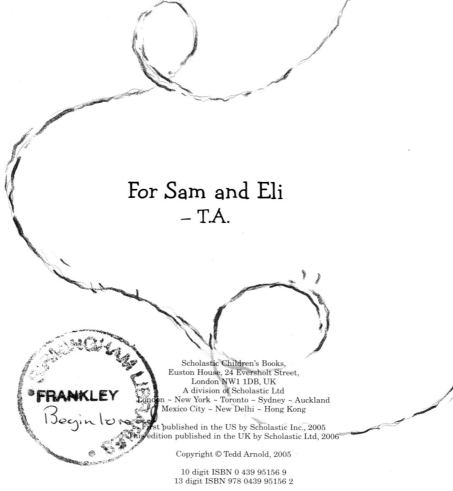

For Sam and Eli
– T.A.

Scholastic Children's Books,
Euston House, 24 Eversholt Street,
London NW1 1DB, UK
A division of Scholastic Ltd
London ~ New York ~ Toronto ~ Sydney ~ Auckland
Mexico City ~ New Delhi ~ Hong Kong

First published in the US by Scholastic Inc., 2005
This edition published in the UK by Scholastic Ltd, 2006

Printed in Singapore

10 9 8 7 6 5 4 3 2 1

Frankley Library
Balaam Wood School, New Street. B45 0EU
Tel: 0121 464 7676

Loans are up to 28 days. Fines are charged if items are not returned by the due date. Items can be renewed at the Library, via the internet or by telephone up to 3 times.
Items in demand will not be renewed.

Date for return		
0 9 JAN 2019		

14

Check out our online catalogue to see what's in stock, renew or reserve books.

www.libraryofbirmingham.com

Like us on Facebook!

Please use a bookmark.